GRANDPA MOLE™ AND COUSIN MOLES'™ JOURNEYS

by

Marjorie Ainsborough Decker

Illustrated by

Theanna

Colleen Murphy Scott

Back Cover Photo by Dave Canaday

A Faith Adventure Book
from **CHRISTIAN MOTHER GOOSE**

CHRISTIAN MOTHER GOOSE™ WORLD
Grand Junction, Colorado   81502

GRANDPA MOLE™ AND
COUSIN MOLES'™ JOURNEYS

CHRISTIAN MOTHER GOOSE™

Un Petit Enfant Les Conduira ™

#1 National Bestseller Author
MARJORIE AINSBOROUGH DECKER

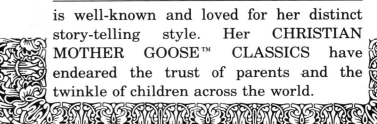

is well-known and loved for her distinct story-telling style. Her CHRISTIAN MOTHER GOOSE™ CLASSICS have endeared the trust of parents and the twinkle of children across the world.

Library of Congress Catalog Card Number: 85-71808
ISBN 0-933724-16-0

Printed in the United States of America.

First Edition   July 1985

Second Edition   November 1985

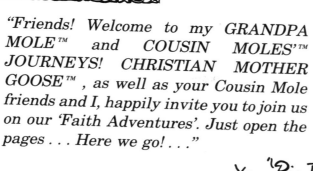

"Friends! Welcome to my GRANDPA MOLE™ and COUSIN MOLES'™ JOURNEYS! CHRISTIAN MOTHER GOOSE™, as well as your Cousin Mole friends and I, happily invite you to join us on our 'Faith Adventures'. Just open the pages . . . Here we go! . . ."

Your "Big Buddy,"
Grandpa Mole

CONTENTS

Today, the charming characters from the growing WORLD OF CHRISTIAN MOTHER GOOSE™ are inspiring families throughout the land with Bestselling books, quality music and audio products, fine gifts, activity programs, video, and now licensed doll and plush toy collectibles.

THE WIG-WAGGY PATH

There's a Wig-Waggy Path
   At the edge of town,
And it leads to the valley
   Down below;
It begins at a fork
   In the road, where two signs
Point the way
   For the travelers, as they go.

It happened, one fine day,
   Cousins Moles reached the fork,
As they rode with a basket
   Full of flutes.
They were off on their way
   Helping dear Grandpa Mole,
When they saw the signs
   Which showed different routes.

Grandpa Mole had told them,
   "Take the sign that says 'Straight',
When you ride with the flutes
   To Dingley Tide.
It won't take very long
   To reach the music shop,
With the flutes I've made
   With hand-crafted pride."

With Noggin at the front,
   And Toggle at the back,
Cousins Moles had stopped
   To take a short rest.
They looked off to the right,
   And looked off to the left,
To decide on the way
   They thought was the best.

6

On the Wig-Waggy Path
   Pretty flowers grew tall,
So it didn't take them long
   To decide
That the Wig-Waggy Path
   Was the prettiest one,
And must lead in the end
   To Dingley Tide!

"Hurray! and off we go
   Down the Wig-Waggy Path!"
All the Cousin Moles
   Were happy to agree.
Noggin, Tilly, Mogie,
   Rimpy, Tolly, too,
With Dolly, and with Toggle,
   Fancy free!

The flowers by the path
   Very soon disappeared;
And prickly thistles
   Sprouted up instead!
As the Wig-Waggy Path
   Took them down, down and down;
Through bends
   And waggy branches overhead.

The moles got thirsty-dry,
   And stopped to get a drink
At a fountain
   In a mossy-green glen.
The fountain, too, was dry,
   So all the little moles
Stayed, oh! so thirsty
   As they rode again.

7

Down deeper on the path,
   They came across a house
Where a man looked out
   A small windowpane.
"Please may we have a drink?"
   Noggin asked, as they stopped;
"We're thirsty, sir,"
   He started to explain.

"Oh, I never go out
   In the rain," said the man,
As he shouted
   Through the small windowpane;
"I might get soaking wet,
   And I might catch a cold;
No, I never will go out
   In the rain."

"But it isn't raining,
   Is it?", said Cousin Moles.
"But it *might*,
   And it's *dangerous* going out!
See all those clouds up there?
   They could rain anytime,
Then you'll get a drink of water,
   There's no doubt."

The thirsty moles rode on,
   Down the Wig-Waggy path,
To a house with some black sheep
   They heard bleat.
The man inside the house
   Said he never comes out,
As he might meet a lion
   In the street!

Tilly, Tolly, Dolly,
   Had tears upon their cheeks;
"We're so thirsty,
   No one cares," they cried;
"And the Wig-Waggy path
   Keeps twisting down and down;
How will we ever get
   To Dingley Tide?"

The boy moles now looked sad,
   So they stopped on the path,
And prayed someone would come
   To help them there.
They looked up hopefully,
   Believing in their hearts:
"Little moles can see
   An answer to their prayer."

8

Up the Wig-Waggy Path
  A kindly man appeared,
With a cane,
  And a water bottle, too.
"I can't believe my eyes!"
  He shouted in surprise,
"A cycle full of moles!
  How do you do?"

"Are you an angel, sir?"
  Whispered all Cousin Moles;
"Will you save us from
  This dry, thirsty state?"
The kindly traveler smiled:
  "An angel, I am not!
I *was* the Crooked Man,
  But now I'm straight!"

"I used to live down here,
  Down the Wig-Waggy Path,
And I walked a crooked mile
  Every day;
But since I read a Book where
  God makes the crooked straight,
They call me Mr. Straight,
  The Water-way!"

"You see, I know the ways
  Of the Wig-Waggy Path,
And this air will make you
  Thirsty, and so dry.
So I come here every day
  To see who needs my help;
And I always bring
  A nice, fresh drink supply."

"A drink! A drink! A drink!"
  Cousin Moles danced about,
As they drank sweet water
  Up to their fill.
"Now, Little Moles, turn back
  Up the Wig-Waggy path,
And I'll help you
  Reach the top of the hill."

So Cousin Moles returned
  Up the Wig-Waggy Path,
With Mr. Straight
  Assisting at their side.
At last they reached the top,
  And the fork in the road,
And took the Straight Path
  Quick! to Dingley Tide!

9

GOD SAID . . .

God said . . . "Light be!"
At once the light was there!
God said . . . "Water!"
And water did appear.

God said . . . "Land, sun,
With moon and stars, now be!"
Straightway they were there,
In shining finery!

God said . . . "Eagles!"
At once they filled the air!
Flying high, to show us
How we can mount up there.

God said . . . "Peace Doves!"
So gentle is their name,
He chose one to alight on Jesus
As the Spirit came.

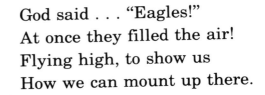

God said . . . "Penguins!"
(I'm glad He wanted those!)
Here they came a-waddling
In their black and white clothes.

God said . . . "Goldfish!"
They answered, "Here we are!"
(I think He knew, some day I'd
Need a few in my jar.)

God said . . . "Apples!"
And apple trees appeared!
They came with seeds in apples,
To grow trees for years and years.

God said . . . "Wheat-grain!"
And right away it grew!
Turning into loaves of bread
For boys and girls like you!

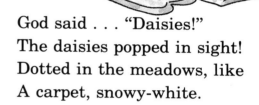

God said . . . "Daisies!"
The daisies popped in sight!
Dotted in the meadows, like
A carpet, snowy-white.

God said . . . "Fireflies!"
At once they came, so bright!
With lamps for tails, to light up
As they fly in the night!

God said . . . "Puppies!"
And there they were with tails!
Ready for a-wagging, like
Some friendly little sails.

God said . . . "Children!
And let them be like Me!"
Oh! I am *glad* He said so –
That's how *I* came to be!

11

FLUTES FOR SEVEN COUSIN MOLES

Grandpa Mole had made a secret present for each of the Cousin Moles . . . a beautiful, hand-made flute!

All over Dandelion Sea, Grandpa Mole was famous for the wonderful flutes he carved and polished. He was a master craftsman at his job.

For months, he had been quietly working on seven special designs.

Now and then, he would picture the little moles up on the bandstand in Polly Woggle Park, performing for the Petals and Praise Concerts each Saturday night.

The praise filled the air with music and song; and the petals filled the air with sweet perfume. Together, they made a lovely cloud to float up to the Lord.

Cousin Moles always sang with all their might at the concerts, but Grandpa Mole thought that learning to play the flute was now the next step for Noggin, Tilly, Mogie, Rimpy, Tolly, Dolly and Toggle Mole.

He had sent a special invitation to Cousin Moles. Charlie Cricket, who delivered the letter, was the only other one who knew what it was all about.

And now the flutes were ready and waiting!

Cousin Moles came bounding up the path to the tree house, just as Grandpa Mole's cuckoo clock cuckooed, "Two!" They looked their very best and had brought a present of their own . . . fresh peas from their pea patch.

"Sit around the table, little friends; close your eyes and then I'll bring in your presents," said Grandpa Mole in great excitement.

Of course, the Cousin Moles sat down very quickly, and shut their eyes till they couldn't see at all!

In front of each little mole, Grandpa Mole gently placed a beautiful, polished flute.

"Now you can look!", he chortled.

"Oh! Grandpa Mole! A flute! . . . A flute! . . . A flute!" All Cousin Moles filled the house with squeals and peals of happy wonder. But when Grandpa Mole raised his hands, they became quiet at once; as they felt that was the most grown-up thing to do when a Cousin Mole had a grown-up, hand-made flute.

"These are the best flutes I have ever made. And I am proud to give them to my dear little friends, the Cousin Moles!" said Grandpa Mole with much affection.

The Cousin Moles cheered to hear him.

"May we play them now?"

"There is no better time than the present to begin something worthwhile," Grandpa Mole assured them.

And that is all it took to make his tree house almost burst with funny music; as if a hundred birds were suddenly learning to sing!

"What are those strange sounds coming from Grandpa Mole's house?" Humpty Dumpty asked Benjamin Bumblebee, as they passed by.

But inside the tree house, Grandpa Mole sat basking in the squeaks and piping of seven Cousin Moles with their very first flutes.

With his eyes closed, all Grandpa Mole could see was his vision of admiring Dandelion Sea creatures, as they listened to Cousin Moles on the bandstand playing so beautifully . . .

"All things bright and beautiful,
All creatures great and small,
All things wise and wonderful,
The Lord God made them all."

13

THE WORLD OF "BELOW-THE-KNEES"

I know a world — not very big —
  You must be small to fit it;
It's called "Below-The-Knees,"
  And I can easily fit in it.

So many little girls and boys
  Come down to meet each day there;
The things we see and find! Oh, we're
  So glad that we can play there!

Yes, you can stop and watch for hours
  The creatures in the grass there;
The little birds and bugs hop, hop,
  To see us as we pass there.

The bigger world, Above-The-Knees,
  Is hurrying and talking;
It's hard for them up there to see
  A furry bug out walking.

I wonder if they know up there
  That if they stopped to hear us,
They'd hear us telling Jesus
  How we love to have Him near us.

Because, down in Below-The-Knees,
  The Lord has made a place there,
For Him and us, and angels, too,
  Who see the Father's face there.

When daylight leaves Below-The Knees,
  We kneel and say our prayers there;
And then Above-The-Knees comes down
  To take us up the stairs there.

LITTLE SHIP

Little ship, I set your sail
    To follow with the winds of God
The course of life The Son of God
    Has laid for you, today.

Little ship, I place aboard
    Your compass and your sacred chart:
God's Word to guide your tender heart
    From sea to sea, each day.

Little ship, the flag you fly
    Flies bravely o'er the waves below;
It bears the Name of Jesus, so
    Your course is safe in Him.

Little ship, sail on, sail on;
    Bring home a cargo, rich and true,
To Him Who gives the Light and Life to you
    To sail; sail on!

        Little ship . . .
           Little ship . . .
               Sail with God!

16

WHO EVER THOUGHT!

Who ever thought,
That feather by feather,
God could put birds
Together, together!

Who ever thought
That by speaking some words,
God could made sky
To hold all of the birds!

BUTTERFLIES AND BUZZING BEES

Butterflies and buzzing bees,
Dandelions dancing in the breeze;
   Little orchids,
    Purple, yellow flowers everywhere!
They all seem to tell me
That God really cares!

Little flowers are full of grace,
Happy with the sun upon their face;
   They just gently grow
    And shed their fragrance everywhere!
They all seem to tell me
That God really cares!

EVERY LITTLE TREE

Every little tree
  Waving merrily,
Sings that "God made me!"
  Happy as can be!
Every little creature sings —
  Ladybugs and leaping frogs
And tiny things with wings.
  All around the world,
Happy songs unfurled,
  Floating up above,
Telling of God's love;
  Singing, singing
One big song:
  "I'm so happy
God loves even me!"

18

PITTER, PATTER BLESSING

If you want to be
  Where God commands
The blessing,
  Then you must stand
All together!
  If you want to be
Where God commands
  The blessing,
Then you must love
  One another!

If you want to bring
  Sweet pleasure
To the Lord,
  Then you must stand
All together!
  If you want the world
To know about
  His love,
Then you must love
  One another!

Pitter, patter, blessing!
Pitter, patter, blessing!
Where God's children
Stand together;
Pitter, patter, blessing!
Pitter, patter, blessing!
When God's children
Love each other.

HOW GOOD, HOW GOOD IS GOD!

A golden sun up in the sky;
  How good, how good is God!
A hundred million stars on high;
  How good, how good is God!
The falling rain to fill the streams;
  How good, how good is God!
A silver moon with kindly beams;
  How good, how good is God!

Rainbows of flowers and bushy trees;
  How good, how good is God!
The singing birds and honey bees;
  How good, how good is God!
The grassy fields and sea-shore sand;
  How good, how good is God!
The wiggly things that sit and stand;
  How good, how good is God!

20

The dancing breeze and juicy fruit;
    How good, how good is God!
The hills that wear a snowy suit;
    How good, how good is God!
A cozy house where we can live;
    How good, how good is God!
All good things He loves to give;
    How good, how good is God!

The loving Saviour, Jesus, came;
    How good, how good is God!
He healed the sick, the blind and lame;
    How good, how good is God!
He loved me so, He died for me;
    How good, how good is God!
He called me to his family;
    How good, how good is God!

He keeps me safe and cares for me;
    How good, how good is God!
Dear Jesus prays in Heaven for me;
    How good, how good is God!
He gave the Bible, so I know,
    How good, how good is God!
Oh, all His world and wonders show
    How good, how good is God!

THE TOMORROW CATCHERS

Once upon a sunny Dandelion Sea day, Grandpa Mole and Cousin Moles . . . yes, all of them . . . Tilly, Tolly, Dolly, Toggle, Noggin, Mogie and Rimpy, met together in the field behind Grandpa Mole's tree house.

They were launching off on an exciting journey. Grandpa Mole's balloon and a friendly wind were waiting to take them to the castle of the Tomorrow Catchers!

Cousins Moles didn't know what to expect when they got there, but all the little moles felt very safe, and knew they would learn wonderful things whenever Grandpa Mole took them on a journey in his balloon.

"One, two, three, four, five, six, seven . . . seven Cousin Moles all safely in the basket," Grandpa Mole called out. Stretching his hands across their heads, he thanked the Lord for a safe journey. At once, the friendly wind lifted them up, high above the tree house.

Brother Rabbit and Bo-Peep ran out to wish them, "Happy Sailing!" Benjamin Bumblebee buzzed his wings from the tip-top of the tree house.

Charlie Cricket, who was delivering letters down Leafy Lane, saw them flying, and shouted, "Do you have the *Today Book*?"

"Yes, we have the *Today Book*," Toggle Mole shouted back. Toggle knew they had it, because he had to stand on it to keep it in place.

"Does *everyone* know where we're going, Grandpa Mole?" asked Tilly.

"It seems as if everyone in Dandelion Sea must know," laughed Grandpa Mole.

In fact, nearly everyone *did* know. It had been the talk of the town for over a week that Cousin Moles were going with Grandpa Mole to the Tomorrow Catchers' Castle.

Once in a while a weather balloon, sent off from the Tomorrow Catchers, would float down into Dandelion Sea. Clusters of villagers would gather to examine it. Everyone wondered what kind of people the Tomorrow Catchers were.

Grandpa Mole was the best one to find out! And Cousin Moles were so proud that he wanted them to go with him . . . although they were not quite sure why.

"Little moles think different things than bigger moles, sometimes," said Noggin, "and I think that's why Grandpa Mole brought us along."

"Why are they called Tomorrow Catchers?" asked Mogie.

"I don't know," replied Noggin.

"Are we Tomorrow creatures?" asked Dolly.

"No, moles are Today creatures, I think," answered Noggin.

Cousin Moles kept squeaking and shouting as they saw new sights down below them.

They sailed over some chipmunks who were having a picnic.

"Look at the basket of moles up there!" one of them cried out.

"Moles are supposed to be in holes, not in balloons," another chipmunk answered.

Rimpy cupped his hands around his mouth and shouted down, "We're going to the Tomorrow Catchers' Castle!"

The chipmunks stopped eating. They were shocked. "They must be brave moles," they said to one another.

When Cousin Moles heard that remark, they smiled big, brave smiles at each other. The balloon sailed on over hills and deep valleys.

"What is the difference between Today and Tomorrow creatures?" Dolly chattered on.

"I don't know. Ask Toggle, he's standing on the *Today Book*," Noggin said with a sigh.

"We can't read it while I'm standing on it," Toggle reminded them.

"It's Grandpa Mole's book, and he knows all about it," Tolly nodded. "He said it's very important, and that's why he brought it today."

"Cushaw! Cushaw." The balloon rose higher. Grandpa Mole looked through his telescope. They were passing over Christian Mother Goose's house. Very quickly they left most of Christian Mother Goose Land behind them.

24

Watching carefully through his telescope, Grandpa Mole suddenly shouted, "There's the castle!".

The little moles became very quiet, as each one peered over the edge of the basket to catch sight of the Tomorrow Catcher's Castle.

"Cushaw! Cushaw!", the balloon began to ease down in a field close to the gates of the stone castle. The countryside around them seemed very, very still.

Grandpa Mole lifted each Cousin Mole out of the basket, then took the big *Today Book* under his arm. "Follow me, and stay together," he reminded them.

So Cousin Moles lined up behind him, just the way they do on their long sepcycle, with Noggin in front and Toggle at the back. They followed obediently to the big iron gate.

The gate was open, and for the very first time, little creatures from Dandelion Sea walked up to the door of the Tomorrow Catchers' Castle.

Grandpa Mole lifted the huge door knocker and banged three times. All Cousin Moles stood behind him, very close, and held their breath.

The great wooden door swung open, and a curly-bearded face peeped at them in surprise.

"Good day, sir," Grandpa Mole greeted him, in an extra friendly fashion. "I'm Matthew Mole from Dandelion Sea, and I've come with Cousin Moles to bring you a gift."

"A gift? Come in, if you please, do come in."

The curly-bearded man led them into a large, stone banquet hall. Four other curly-beards were sitting around a long table, studying old, big books.

"Five Curly-Beards live here!" thought Grandpa Mole, as Curly-Beard One introduced them:

"This is the Mole family from Dandelion Sea. I thought it would save time if they met us all at once."

Curly-Beard Two looked up and said, "We'll call you 'Mr. Mole' and 'Little Moles', so that we won't have to waste time remembering your names."

"Of course, of course, of course," said Curly-Beard Three.

"We haven't told him our names yet," whispered Tolly to Dolly.

"Then how can he forget to remember what he doesn't know?" Dolly whispered back.

"Perhaps it has something to do with being a Tomorrow Catcher," hinted Tilly.

"We need all the time we can get for the study of catching tomorrow," said Curly-Beard Four.

"Yes, we keep our minds set on that goal of catching tomorrow," said Curly-Beard Five.

"Catching tomorrow?" asked Noggin slowly. He was standing underneath the *Today Book* that Grandpa Mole was holding, and felt safe to speak from there.

"It's gratifying to see little moles interested in such a deep study as 'tomorrow'," murmured Curly-Beard Four.

"You are the first moles ever to come through our gates," mumbled Curly-Beard Five as he thumbed through a yellowed, old book.

Curly-Beard One beckoned them to sit down.

The table was almost as long as the room, and there were plenty of chairs all around it, but Cousin Moles crowded all together on one side. Grandpa Mole took the empty chair at one end of the table. He placed the *Today Book* in front of him.

"Ah! You seem to have brought some important literature with you, Mr. Mole," said Curly-Beard Two.

"Undoubtedly, it deals with the subject of Tomorrow?" inquired Curly-Beard Four.

"Quite the contrary," answered Grandpa Mole, trying hard to remember some of his very best words. "It is called the *Today Book*."

"Today!" All five Tomorrow Catchers closed their big books with a bang! Dust flew everywhere.

Curly-Beard Five stood up. "Mr. Mole, look above you."

Grandpa Mole, along with all the Cousin Moles, strained his head back as far as it could go to look all around the high walls.

For the first time, they saw a row of giant butterfly nets hanging across the top of each wall. They looked like rows of still flags, with brightly colored banners attached to each one.

"Those are the nets of honor from former Tomorrow Catchers," Curly-Beard Five continued. "Households who spent their lives in the pursuit of tomorrow. As all creatures should know, time has wings; and time flies! So we have made the finest butterfly nets, and built the best hourglass in the land, so that we can see the last grain of sand at that magic moment when tomorrow flys by."

"We have only that one moment in which to catch tomorrow," said Curly-Beard One, solemnly. "And we prepare every day in the hope of catching it. Our task is difficult, as we must try each night to catch Tomorrow in the dark. You may stay and watch if you wish."

Cousin Moles all breathed out, "Oh . . ." in one sound. The thought of staying up late, and watching Tomorrow Catchers, almost took their breath away.

"We have little time for eating and resting, Mr. Mole, but you will find simple food in the cushion room. You may rest there till midnight." Then leading all the moles, Curly-Beard One took them upstairs to a room full of cushions.

Grandpa Mole shared the simple food between them.

"Please don't forget to wake us up, will you, Grandpa Mole?" asked the Cousin Moles sleepily.

Grandpa Mole nodded. And Cousin Moles fell fast asleep.

At a quarter to twelve, the Tomorrow Catchers knocked on the door. Try as he would, Grandpa Mole could not wake up even one little mole. They were snuggled in the cushions, with just their noses sticking out, and he knew they wouldn't wake up till morning.

Grandpa Mole quietly followed the Tomorrow Catchers to the roof of the castle. A balcony surrounded it. Tiny bits of moonlight helped him see better in the dark.

The biggest hourglass he had ever seen stood on a pedestal. Only a little sand was left in the top, as it slowly trickled through the narrow neck to the bottom.

Curly-Beard One held a lantern by the hourglass. All the other Curly-Beards leaned over the balcony with their butterfly nets ready. Everything was silent.

Suddenly, Curly-Beard One loudly shouted, "Now!" and the swish of the nets sent a wind whistling over Grandpa Mole's head!

"I caught it! I caught it!" Curly-Beard Five cried out. The strange sound of whirring and flapping shook his net wildly.

The other Tomorrow Catchers rushed to his side. Grandpa Mole stood quietly watching.

In great excitement, the lantern shone upon the shaking net. Two bright eyes stared back. "An owl . . . an owl . . ." all Curly-Beards sighed, in sorrowful tones. "Tomorrow has eluded us again."

In a leather book they marked the 365,233 times the long line of Tomorrow Catchers had failed to catch tomoroow.

In single file they went down the stairs. "Good Night," Grandpa Mole said softly, as he opened the door to the cushion room.

29

The next morning, Cousin Moles woke up before Grandpa Mole. They tickled him till he woke up laughing.

"It's tomorrow," they shouted.

"No, it's today," Grandpa Mole chuckled. And before they could ask him why they never saw the Tomorrow Catchers at work, he told them all about the happenings at midnight.

For breakfast they had the same food as the night before: bread, water and fruit.

The Tomorrow Catchers were already studying their old, old books when the moles stepped into the great hall. Grandpa Mole sat down by the *Today Book*, and Cousin Moles stood around him.

"Good Morning," the moles said, with smiling voices.

The Tomorrow Catchers looked up with weary faces.

"We are very tired today . . . very tired," they said. "You must realise how wearing it is, staying up late each night in the hope of catching Tomorrow."

"Why do you keep trying?" asked Grandpa Mole. "What benefits will there be?"

"Ah . . . to catch Tomorrow would give us untold benefits. Caught in the safety of our net, we could face Tomorrow. It would be in our hands. We would have no fear of Tomorrow then," Curly-Beard Five spoke longingly.

"You do not count Tomorrow as a friend, then?" Grandpa Mole questioned him.

30

"No! We must beware of Tomorrow. And be on our guard. And anticipate its demands and schemes." The Tomorrow Catchers spoke all at once, in trembling voices.

"Gentlemen, I have here the *Today Book* . . . brought as a gift for you," Grandpa Mole told them kindly.

"A gift! . . . for us?" The Curly-Beards stood up in surprise, and shuffled to Grandpa Mole's end of the table. "No one has ever brought us a gift before."

Grandpa Mole opened the *Today Book* and began to read: "Surely *goodness* and *mercy* shall follow me all the *days* of my life . . . So teach us to number our *days* . . . Every *day* will I bless Thee . . . This is the *day* that the *Lord* has made, and we will rejoice and be glad in it!"

"That big book is all about Today?" asked the astonished Tomorrow Catchers.

"Every page," smiled Grandpa Mole. "Thousands of wise sayings, all about Today: and most of them from the Lord's own Great Book."

"What does He say about Tomorrow in His Great Book?" all the Curly-Beards wanted to know.

"It is the *Lord* who holds tomorrow! That's why you cannot catch it. But He has given you Today, a moment at a time, in your own hand. His hand reaches out to you each day. And if you will hear His voice, it must be *Today*! That is why the *Today Book* is so precious, and why we brought it as a gift for you."

Grandpa Mole handed the *Today Book* to the Tomorrow Catchers, and they sat down with the book between them, looking at each other.

"Today comes with the Lord's best upon it. Take it as your friend; live with it; laugh with it; love with it; then you'll have no fear of tomorrow."

As Cousin Moles stood listening, they grinned till you could hardly see their eyes. They were so proud of Grandpa Mole!

Yes, they had really been in the Tomorrow Catchers' Castle . . . and they had seen the great butterfly nets . . . and they knew about the fine hourglass . . . and the owl . . . and best of all, they had seen the Tomorrow Catchers carefully studying the *Today Book* as the castle door closed behind them.

Off to the balloon they skipped and ran. "Hurray! we're going back to Dandelion Sea Today!" they shouted.

"Hurray! for Today!" chuckled Grandpa Mole, as the balloon wheezed, "Cushaw! Cushaw!" and took them sailing home.

THE TENDERTUFF PLANT

Grandpa Mole and Christian Mother Goose were enjoying an afternoon of bird-watching — and bird listening!

Chickadees were whistling at their best; the wood thrush would sing no less than a full concert; after which the wrens would pipe: "Cheery, cheery, cheery."

Not to be left out, the woodpeckers would drum, "Wick-a-wack, wick-a-wack, wick-a-wack!" And whenever there was a moment's silence, the mockingbirds would imitate all the others.

"The time of the singing of birds is come," laughed Christian Mother Goose.

Grandpa Mole nodded in agreement as he swept his telescope around the countryside. "That's a strange sight," he mused, fixing his gaze across Cousin Moles' pea patch.

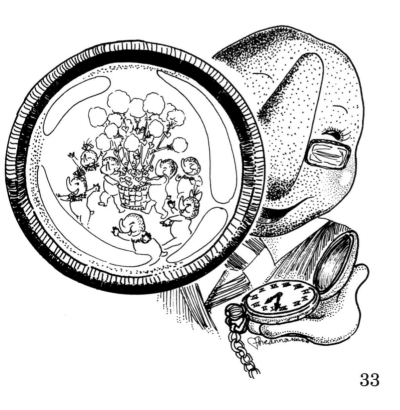

"A new bird?" asked Christian Mother Goose eagerly.

"No, but I do say it's a new sight for Cousin Moles. Look at their antics!"

Noggin and Toggle were holding a giant plant, while the rest of Cousin Moles ran around them in great excitement.

"That's the first one they've ever seen," chuckled Grandpa Mole. "And I vouch those little moles will be here within two minutes to ask us about it." He took out his pocket watch to check the time.

In less than two minutes, Tilly, Tolly, Dolly, Mogie, and Rimpy were running and jumping around Christian Mother Goose, while Noggin and Toggle stood proudly holding the giant plant.

"What is it? What is it?" they kept shouting.

"We've never seen one of these before!"

"We found it in the pea patch today."

"If everyone will sit down, we'll tell you about it," Grandpa Mole promised.

Immediately, all Cousin Moles sat down, as quiet as could be.

"This is a most unusual plant, and the only one of it s kind. A long time ago, Christian Mother Goose and I learned a wonderful story about it."

"Tell them the story, Grandpa Mole," urged Christian Mother Goose.

The little moles drew close around the storyteller as he began:

"Off in the valley of Bethgali-Buff,
  Grows the mysterious plant, Tendertuff!
The Tendertuff plant is remarkable stuff;
  Its wonderful tales can't be told oft enough.

Some say it began as a single, small seed;
  Nobody noticed; and no one gave heed;
Till one sunny day, on a dry, barren bluff,
  Appeared the white wonder they call "Tendertuff".

So soft and gentle, it looked to the eye,
  As if it would blow with the wind to the sky.
The town called it "Tender" — and tried with a puff
  To blow it away; but Tender was tough!

35

So, Tendertuff then was its lasting name;
  And in a short time it had gained much fame.
I'll tell just a few of the tales and the ways
  That Tendertuff won all the villagers' praise.

It happened one year, as the Tendertuff spread,
  The harvest was short, and there wasn't much bread;
Till someone discovered a secret so sweet —
  That Tendertuff seeds were exactly like wheat!

Thousands and thousands of starry seed pods
  Poured out their seeds with the touch of a rod.
Laughing and shouting came each neighborhood:
  "Taste of the Tendertuff seeds, Oh how good!"

When water was scarce from the shortage of rain,
  The Tendertuff stems were all found to contain
Gallons of water, so fresh to the taste
  That everyone filled up their barrels with haste.

Soon all of the children were laid down to rest
   On soft downy pillows of Tendertuff's best
Feathery tips, of the whitest of white,
   Which gave them the nicest of sleep every night.

The children all know it's a mystery deep,
   How Tendertuff always lights up when they sleep.
So now all the children as they go to bed,
   Will carry a Tendertuff candle, instead!

They love its sweet smell, and they love its soft glow,
   As they kneel to thank God for loving them so.
"God bless dear Mommy and Daddy," and then
The Tendertuff nods as each child says, "Amen."

There's really no end to the blessings you'll find
   In the Tendertuff plant; it's one of a kind!
Yet from one small seed, I've good news to report:
   That Tendertuff's spreading by land and seaport.

No weather or soil in the worst of condition
   Can stop Tendertuff from its kind, healing mission.
It takes root wherever a crack lets it in;
   Then Tendertuff blessings sprout up and begin. . .

37

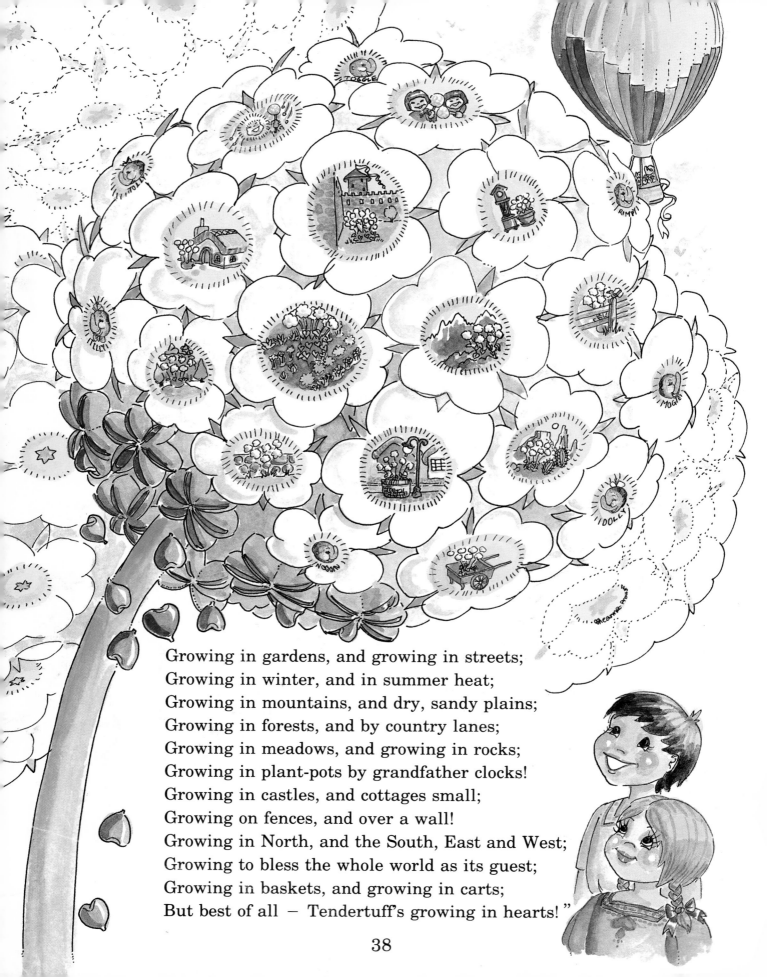

Growing in gardens, and growing in streets;
Growing in winter, and in summer heat;
Growing in mountains, and dry, sandy plains;
Growing in forests, and by country lanes;
Growing in meadows, and growing in rocks;
Growing in plant-pots by grandfather clocks!
Growing in castles, and cottages small;
Growing on fences, and over a wall!
Growing in North, and the South, East and West;
Growing to bless the whole world as its guest;
Growing in baskets, and growing in carts;
But best of all — Tendertuff's growing in hearts! "